CW01501547

THEY COME IN DIFFERENT SHAPES AND SIZES

Sarah Loutfi

MINERVA PRESS
WASHINGTON   LONDON   MONTREUX

THEY COME IN DIFFERENT SHAPES AND SIZES
Copyright ©Sarah Loutfi 1996

ISBN 1 86106 205 2

First Published 1996 by
MINERVA PRESS
195 Knightsbridge
London SW7 1RE

Printed in Great Britain
B.W.D. Ltd, Northolt, Middlesex

THEY COME IN DIFFERENT SHAPES AND SIZES

Contents

"Cages come in different shapes and sizes, bank-shaped some of them."

Bert in *Mary Poppins*
by P.L. Travers

Asylum Madness

Rocking slowly, to and fro, with his arms wrapped tightly about him, the room looked bare. Snow-white walls struck the dark outlines of his body, reflecting their fairy tale falseness in his dark eyes. To and fro, back and forth, calm and steady, it helped him think, of his inner strength. Of mind.

There was a fly, buzzing about the room. Settling here and there then, on his nose. He began to boil; his arms wrenched behind him made it difficult to swipe.

One, two, his head thrown about in a fit of frustration, the fly resettled again and again; he, with his shoulders twisting, his limbless torso, thrusting his neck out in an agony of frustrated confused irritation. He screamed.

Echoes of anger that vibrated against the walls of his soft, pearly tomb. Rocking frantically, he yelled again as the insect touched his face in taunting jest.

The door flung open.

The pendulum stopped, he sank to the floor. Her long coat hid the evil within, but it was white. It had to be. To match the walls.

He looked up in fear, for the fly had disappeared. He could see the light bouncing gaily off the needle that she held in her grip.

"Come on Mr —."

Her eyes unmoved, uncaring. She stepped toward him.

With a thud he fell to the floor. The fly could pester him for days and days, he would not move.

And by the light of the now luminous white walls. She looked mad.

War

Over a table, the men in ties grin in greedy grimaces at each other. "Your move."

In the streets, the rocks are breaking people's backs as bullets are fired. The gunmen sneer and climb a step. But the men in ties are far higher.

"Your move."

The people stagger under the weight. BANG! A gunman falls, the people smile, then cower in fear as the man in a tie frowns.

"Ku Klux Klan," and the rocks are blown away along with the carriers. The table sways as gold coins hit it with sudden force. A man in a tie laughs out loud.

"Checkmate."

People like ants run to and fro, dodging bullets as each gunman smirks at another catch. The table is bending as the coins get heavier. And the men with guns only ever climb one step, then they drop. Dead.

The squashed flies hit the smart man's spectacles, making bloodstains on the glass. He lifts a hand and wipes them away in disgust.

The table breaks under the weight of the coins. The board smashes on the floor. Everything is silent.

The men in ties have filled their pockets, so they leave the room, looking for another game.

Courtroom Drama

Seated upon a throne of generous orange crates and bloodied superiority, he grinned down at them.

"Violence!" he cried. "Violence is a sin."

Forced to look up at him, she stood her ground, the words of truth he would never hear. In her mind. She sensed her power, a power far stronger than his. The power to change, to stop the way things were, for good.

Knowing this, he came down hard on her.

"You will stand up," he screamed. He was fearful of her presence and worried by her strength.

Calmly resisting, she took hold of her seat, her eyes fixed on him, and she spoke with a defiant smile that shattered the glass window which had been erected to separate the privileged from the angry.

"Violence," he sobbed. "Violence, is you. You. Violence, is disobedience."

While in the green fields not so far away, the machines worked by robots ploughed and pillaged the land and the life that she had loved.

"Violence, is rebellion and riot," he gasped, shivering and shaking as she remained seated, depriving him of the vital authority he needed to keep him upright.

Her eyes wandered from his to the world outside, where houses were ransacked and the people thrown out, where trees stood weeping over ashen valleys. Where mountains struggled to proudly stand, staggering and limping as wounds and gashes were stolen from their sides.

She had broken the rules once. Once, after years of fury, she had defied the man who had told her how to live her life. Now they were all that was left, just the ruler and the rebel. Alone, in a room blanketed by the silence of fear. She sighed and broke it.

"Stop this," she said in a weary expression of experience and anger. "Leave us alone." She rose and left the room, leaving him guiltily subdued by the power of her presence.

9

She will look through the window each day to find him in his loneliness and shrug it off – her world now free, she has no need to argue. He had fought her unfairly with hypocrisy on his side, with fear on his team, and greed at his every command. He held the power of authority in his hand and watchdogs to keep her from his conscience.

All that aside, she had won. Her world had begun, and they had started to rebuild their lives. And to repair the whole senseless mess that he had caused.

Charity

Hunger bit its knifelike jaws into his pleading stomach as his eyes widened, begging for food to nourish it. Groping and grasping at the piles of dirt scattered about him, his face creased. He was trying to cry.

She bent down towards him, thrusting a microphone into his face.

"Oh, the poor dear."

"I'm so sorry, have a biscuit?"

Despairingly, he turned away, concentrating solely on a beetle that crawled slowly past.

" We're here to help people like D— here," she smiled.

"I know he would love to say a big thank you to you lovely viewers."

In anger, snatching the microphone, he opened his mouth to speak. To voice his own opinion.

"But sadly, we don't really have time," she giggled as the camera returned to her grinning face. 'In her land she would be a hero,' he thought.

She worked hard, no one could deny it. Standing on her platform of moral superiority, she giggled again.

"Help him, to understand, oh Lord. Lord, help him to help himself." Which the audience applauded, and they threw their hard-earned wages on to the stage.

The curtains rose and she took a bow. Laughing and smiling, she spoke for the last time.

"I love you all."

She left the stage, ignoring his fallen smile as the relief helicopter flew helplessly in, guided by the roar of guns and weaponry.

Litter

He strolled along the street. The day was quite cold but he felt cosy in his scarf and thick duffel coat. He made sure that he was wrapped up. As he breathed, clouds of mist swirled around his red face. Jokingly, he placed a pretend cigarette to his mouth and blew. He carried on walking, his mind now freshened. He decided to take a longer route than he had originally planned. This way led through a deserted back lane, quite different from the busy, smoky town he was used to.

He entered from the bottom, stopping every five yards to admire the scenery. Old broken bottles were strewn carelessly across patches of earth, cans, tins, clothes, even spare car parts had been thrown disrespectfully on the ground. Then, almost breaking his heart, he saw a little weed poking its pretty green head out between a spongy mattress and an oil can.

A loud screech stirred him from his pity. Behind him were two ginger tomcats. They hissed, backs arched. Their eyes narrowed menacingly as they glared at each other. He stared as they circled, not moving their eyes to disturb the glance of hatred. One spat, stretching out a claw and swiping it cleanly across the other's face. Then the fight began; there seemed to be an orange blur as they tore at one another, hissing, spitting, grimacing. He just looked on, gazing in disbelief as the two ripped and scratched for no apparent reason. Stepping forward, he approached them. His foot crunched heavily on the gravel. They stopped fighting, ears pricked, attentively looking for any sign of danger. When all was clear, they resumed the match, squealing and crying for mercy.

He placed one shoe in between the two ginger clouds and pulled them forcibly apart, using his hands. It took all his strength but finally he managed to separate them. He spoke, questioningly, "Why do this to each other?" The cats looked at him, then at each other, then with a sudden burst of energy, they wrenched themselves free. Caterwauling and screaming once more polluted the air.

He stood still for a minute or two, watching. Then, pulling back the hair that had fallen out of place, he turned to walk back down the lane. Treading carefully, he picked up the broken bottles. Smiling coolly, he removed the tin cans and old clothes, placing them into his bag. He freed the lone weed and, on lifting the gangrenous mattress, he discovered a family of greenery all waiting desperately for the sun to shine. He carried on like this, down the lane, clearing, cleaning, freeing and rescuing when he noticed something.

The screeching had stopped. He turned once more to face the lane where the fighting cats had scrambled. Grinning with satisfaction, he glanced momentarily at the empty, now green, lane.

The Politician

He rose from his seat with the two of them at his side. Walking slowly, he waved as he passed the people. Two plastic pins held up the false smile on his face. The teeth he showed were worn, from their continual use for deception.

As he mounted the platform, the people were forced to cheer, their arms waving and clapping unwillingly, through iron bars. Once behind the altar, the two left his side. He began to shake, quiver, tremble.

It was from here that he had to speak. The paper in his hand shook violently with his every word. Talking endlessly, about order, he shouted with fickle passion.

"I want a land of freedom, world freedom."

Yet, as he spoke, whilst all eyes were concentrated on his, no one saw his left foot, repeatedly, stamping and grinding on the hands of homeless children. No one saw his right foot, engaged heavily in signing death orders and legal massacre documents.

"Equality for all, education for our children and peace to the nation." Whilst in schools children sat, deprived of their own creativity, and fed the verbiage that 'democracy' ordered them to consume.

Each time he made a statement his feet worked harder: ordering, demanding, killing, oppressing. His lips were moving so fast that no one could comprehend his language, but it didn't matter – they all knew what he was saying.

"I don't want war, really, I love people," he cried as crocodile tears poured down his face like the 'I cry, I walk, I even pick my nose' dolls that he promoted.

People were made angry by him. Not many, just a few. Together they decided to stop the others from cheering, to stop enslaving themselves to a plastic culture, to feel proud instead of being made to feel guilty and responsible for world suffering. They stood together and organised themselves. With broken iron bars, they faced him.

His voice weakened as he saw them; calling feebly for the robots in uniform, he commanded: "Help me."

Out they came, each identical to the other, punching and beating wildly, trying to disperse the crowd. But they were outnumbered by far. As the group advanced, the plastic pins snapped and his teeth fell out. "I love you, all of you, really, with your love and obedience I can help you."

The tears were real now, and, stepping backwards, he trod again on the hand of a child.

After a short while all that was left on the platform was a mechanical recorder that spoke entirely to itself.

"I am your friend, I love you, please obey me, I love you, please obey..."

Native Resistance

"We're not leaving," they said, arms folded, their feet firmly implanted, chained to the earth. All around them mountains rolled, leaves rustled and majestic creatures roamed free, loving and living in gentle harmony with the people and their land.

An unreal claw enticed them with promises of a plastic paradise where children went hungry to the tune of never-ending merry-go-rounds and creatures lay bound in chains to be ridiculed. Where all were depressed in wretched agony, trying to wrench off the smiling masks manufactured for them by humans, who looked alike.

"We're not leaving." Linked by their mutual love, they stood strong. For a while. Their faces reflected the way of life they had led: good, productive, respectful.

Arm in arm they didn't weaken, despite the efforts it made in vain to move them. An evil eye surveyed the area, dreaming dangerously of golden trees, silver grass, an emerald sun and blood-red rivers.

One by one they fell. It was crippling them. The bullets of greed only filled them with rage. Each body was taken and placed in a cage, a plastic cage, with net curtains. Far away from their land.

Tears fell and hearts broke. Thoughtlessly snapped like the beautiful shell of a snail crushed by a bulldozer. Tired of crying, many stayed behind bars, trying to mend their hearts. Others wiped away their sorrow, not with a hand, but with a fist. Clenched. In new-found strength, they broke the bars and burned the cages. Joined by others from meaningless upbringings, they began to rise.

Once on their feet, they saw the land again. Torn and scarred, it cried out for help.

And the claw turned from its barbaric altar, to face an angry people who now stood once more. Together.

Divide And Rule

They are sitting in a group laughing and talking. To each other. It sourly glares at them and gives a supercilious nod to a white-aproned dog standing to attention in the corner,

Bang! A barrier hits the ground with a thud. In the centre of the group.

'Ding a ling!'

A bell rings as the people take their places. On either side of the square. In one corner, half the group stands: backs arched, fangs bared, eyes glaring.

'Ding a ling!'

It wheels itself to the window to watch the match through the glass. It can't walk, for it's grown too fat.

'Round twenty-one.'

The two groups back off. They are turning handles with their feet and punching with their hands. As the handles turn wheels grind, forming neatly printed notes that arrive packaged wastefully at its door.

'Ding a ling a ling.'

Blood now covers the square. The groups turn on each other, dog against bitch, bulldog versus Rottweiler. All scratching with outstretched claws at each other's faces.

'Round four.'

It can't stand the sight of blood, but it can't wheel itself away. Eager bow-tied spaniels do the job for it, each receiving a pat on the head.

The packages keep arriving at the door, whilst, in the square, the battle continues.

Until a battered fighter turns his head to look through its window.

One of the notes arrive at its door, crumpled.

The Businessman

He got up.   Clockwork-minded, he did not think of it as being another day.   He pulled on his trousers and fumbled around for a shirt.

Once dressed, he went into the bathroom.   The toothbrush was in its usual place, in the rack.   He picked it up and placed it inside his mouth.   To the beat of the ever-ticking watch in his head, he brushed his teeth.   One, two, one, two, but as soon as the strokes became rhythmical, musical even, he put it down.

The kitchen was small and, as he sat alone eating, he felt strange. He had never felt like this before and he didn't understand.

The feeling didn't go away.   It stayed with him as he waved her goodbye and set off in his car.   It failed to go as he placed his briefcase by his side.   It was there all the time he travelled and didn't stop until he realised what it was.

Entering the building, he tried to shake it off.   Aloud, he spoke his thoughts, "I'm not allowed to feel, for God's sake, who wants emotion."   But the emotion he felt inside resisted all his attempts to rid himself of it.

He sat alone, again, at his desk.   For ever typing and calling people.   Long distance.   After about an hour he had made over forty phone calls, yet he hadn't spoken to anyone.   The eleven o'clock tea lady poked her head round the door.   "Anything you need?"

"Oh, a cup of tea please," he said, hoping that she would take a long time over it.   Handing him the tea, she turned to go, her back facing him.   "Don't go, please.   Please, stay here."   Embarrassed by what he'd said, he turned away.   She left the room.

Returning to his original position, he put his head in his hands.   He knew what the persistent banging feeling was inside him.   He was very unhappy.   Working all day, every day, with no one beside him. Making the same phone calls, eating the same lunch, going to and fro every day.   Slaving every day for what money couldn't buy.

'I AM NOT A DOG,' he thought, the tears now freely pouring down his face. 'I AM NOT A MACHINE OR A ROBOT, I AM A

18

LIVING HUMAN BEING AND I AM BORED. I am sick of this mechanical existence. How can anyone class how I live as success?'

Grabbing desperately at the phone for a listening ear, pulling open doors to find people, he became wild: "I can't live like this any more!"

But there was no one to hear, see or care.

Education

They were all marched in. Chattering voices filled the room as little people spoke in hushed tones to each other, whilst standing in line, to attention.

The teachers sat on big chairs along the side of the hall, searching the rows of children for an offender. Someone who was talking, eating, laughing.

As he strode in, the hall fell silent. Conversation was suffocated, stifled, with each step. He smiled with authority.

"Today we will learn about obedience."

His eyes narrowed and he bent his neck forward, thrusting it, like a giraffe, into the front line. The medals on his chest glistened in the sunlight.

"And so you must all learn to be silent and accept all that is fed to you: argument is a moral sin."

The children, not knowing any better, nodded their heads simultaneously.

The bell rang and all the pupils were drilled and let out to 'play'. A figure stood at the corner of the playground beating a drum. The children played to the drum, marched to the drum. As the whistle blew, they stood, once more, to attention.

Again the chatter ceased, and tongues dropped from palates and sank in fear to the bottom of mouths.

But one child was smiling. A teacher cried out as if in pain: "Stop smiling."

The child's sneer deepened and his teeth, white regulation teeth, filed to exactly three centimetres in diameter, began to show. He was laughing.

A procession paraded into the playground, the Head leading. His face was determined. Hiding his fear, the Head grabbed the child.

"Shut up," he growled.

At the windows faces appeared, squeezing their heads between the bars, waiting anxiously for the shout. They all knew what was going to happen.

"Atten-shun."

The children's heels clicked together with precision. And the child giggled on.

"Present arms."

Each child lifted a satchel and placed it militarily on their left shoulder. The child was in hysterics, rolling on the floor, tears streaming freely down his cheeks.

"Fire."

And the rebel was silenced.

The 'Woman' Market

She smiled. Her scrubbed, sore, plastic teeth shone falsely in the light. Her eyes creased and her lashes crumpled and fell to the floor.

The heat was unbearable, but her teeth remained fixed, in an unchangeable grimace; her wooden legs were burning.

She began to move, her arms sweating uncontrollably under coats of 'Lovely Limbs' foundation cream. Feet like rocks, squashed, misshapen, forced into tiny ballet shoes.

So that she could dance

The sun shone and the glass magnifies the heat.

"Help me."

She is melting: her lips begin to run and her cheeks sag under the weight of the continual grin.

He points at her.

"Look what you've done to yourself."

And he feeds her spoonfuls of 'Slimfast'.

"So concerned about the way she looks."

His back turns on a fat lady in the corner.

"Get up, you silly girl."

But she can't stand, or sit.

He mops up the plastic puddle with a coloured magazine.

Untitled

"Well then, I'll begin," she said, her eyes beaming down at us from her seat under the apple tree. "Now today, we'll hear a story that's a change from the usual." Settling back into her chair, she raised her eyes to the sky, looking at the leaves that fell from the branches of her shade. "And if any of you are frightened, you must call out. Call out and I'll end the story.

"Once upon a time there lived a little girl, a little girl called Rose. Rose spent much of her time in a little wood not so very far from here." She paused. "If any of you are frightened, you must shout out, because anything you don't like you must abolish.

"Now, one day, Rose decided that she would go for a swim in the lake near her village. She took a towel and her costume and a little brush in the shape of a hedgehog that her grandfather had carved for her. On reaching the river, Rose put down her towel and brush and looked into the water. A smiling girl's face reflected hers and she waved. The water rippled as if in reply and as the river seemed to accept her presence, so Rose felt it would be fine for her to swim. First, she dipped the tip of her toe into the water to test it. A little chill ran up her spine: it was too cold. All of a sudden, a tingly sensation crept up her back and all over her body, and, with a cry of fear, the first in her life, she felt herself being lifted up. Up through the clouds high, breaking branches off her sisters to keep down, pulling at her little bird friends' wings and kicking wildly at the wind.

"When at last she woke up, she found that she had dropped on to a soft pile. Rummaging about to stabilise herself, she noticed and then was hit by a stench so putrid that it brought tears to her eyes, poor dear.

"Do you know what a rubbish pile is?" she asked us, her eyes searching ours for an answer. "It is a big pile of old things that nobody wants or is going to give back to the earth so they throw it on the ground." One girl at the back began to cry.

"On getting away from the horrid heap, Rose walked down a cobbled path, only to see her winged friends in cages and dogs with string tied round their necks. Metal machines roamed the streets, knocking down children and killing the clouds, ruining the breath of life. Humans fought with each other, feeling no remorse at the death of their fellow people. Men with great ripping saws tore at her brother trees and gashed them apart, leaving young chicks homeless and squirrels hungry. In the towns, she saw huge brick buildings with iron fences around them. She encountered a word she'd never seen before: PRIVATE. She saw people through etched glass windows of the big houses, sitting laughing and eating while people lay, disease-ridden, begging on the streets for money. As she walked down the streets, men jeered at her, whistling and slobbering as if she was some kind of usable object, with no self-respect or dignity. Her lips trembled as she saw men in uniforms with wooden sticks, beating and punching innocent people. She saw the guiltless people, flung into a dark hovels with bars at the windows.

"Sick people were left to die, poor people rotted in poverty, women were oppressed, animals were tortured and slaughtered, children brainwashed into robots, cultures mocked, freedom scorned. But worse still, worse than all that cruelty put together, she saw a fat man sitting alone on a pile of banknotes, laughing at all the destruction."

At this point, the children began to call out, "No more grandmother, no more, you're frightening us: end the story now! No more."

"If you don't want to hear the end, run off now and play, and don't worry. Be thankful that life is not that way here. It is up to you to make sure that it never ever goes that way. Go on, run along now."

She carried on talking to herself, unaware that I sat alone listening.

"Rose ran for her life, but could not get back to her home. Left alone, she felt scared and isolated. On entering a place of drinking and merriment, an odd scene in this world, she approached a table. Around it were seated men, women and children like herself, all talking and laughing with each other. Do you know what hope she felt? What immense hope she held inside for the future? No, of course you don't, but her heart was warmed, causing her to smile when a man saw her enter the room. Stretching over the tables, he held out his worn but kindly hand.

"'Welcome comrade.'"

Poppies With Pride

A screen lit up, their eyes followed. Each flicker was reflected in their gormless stares. No brick, bullet or bomb could disturb their intense mesmerised gaze.

In a land far away a tear slowly fell down a human face. Her eyes had not settled upon a coloured screen, but on the window. The green fields, grass and blossoming trees were captured and frozen, as in a photograph, in the back of her mind.

As the screen babbled and prattled the pounds rolled in, like wheels of fortune. Tumbling clumsily, through a big oak door marked 'PRIVATE'.

The tears fell, spitting and pattering like rainfall, landing delicately on the soft leaves of her open book. A book with no cartoons, no jokes, no comedy.

The door marked 'PRIVATE' shook and rattled like a wild bull. Any contrary movement made it shiver – as if in fear? Coins crashed against it like waves, and the foam of white notes fluttered, like birds, around the room.

Now a tiny pool had formed, her clothes were wet: she certainly looked funny. They all laughed, what fun! The smiling teeth were only there as a dam to prevent tears from flowing.

Once more, bullets and bombs fell like cats and dogs on the people outside, but their screams couldn't be heard. They had to be watched.

I couldn't see the door marked 'PRIVATE' any more: the entire oak masterpiece had been covered by the blind coins, not to mention the abundance of white notes, hoarding armaments and polishing rifles. Now at the top of the heap of circular metal pieces, just above those birds of crackling white paper, in fact on the front of the big oak door marked 'PRIVATE', there is a red poppy, pinned to the wood.

The Illusion

He placed it lovingly on the wooden mantelpiece. A creator's joy, it glistened beautifully as the sun hit its edge. All who visited adored it.

"My, what a vase! How much?"

"How beautiful! Look at that crystal!"

One comment lingered, sugar-like, in his memory.

"That'll bring you happiness."

Which was exactly what he thought.

And so it stood, brilliantly, finely polished, reflecting all the room in a silvery glow. He talked to it, confiding in it to guide him, and he made sure that no one came near it.

For fear it might break.

However, one day, a friend came to visit, just to see him. An old friend, a good friend, a close friend. This friend was amazed at the glamorous object that beamed out at him from the end of the room.

"Goodness, how lovely, may I?"

On saying this, the friend touched the side of the glass. He rushed out to protect it.

"No, no, no. Anything, touch anything at all in the room, but not that. I beg of you."

"Please," said the friend. "I promise you the moon in exchange for just one little tiny... touch."

"Very well," he replied. "I only ask you to be very careful."

That was all it took. The vase broke, handled by clumsy fingers.

He fell to his knees, picking up the pieces with limp hands.

He mended it well. But the crack still remained.

Take Us To The Zoo

"Well, who wants to go?" she asked them, her eyes looking kindly upon the group of children. Raising their hands, they remembered the words of others, who had told them how good it was. They paid out cheques for thousands of pounds. Money they didn't have.

The day came and they all got on the bus. As they travelled, grey blocks, pollution and roads tormented them as they went. No one was around; they would see life and greenery soon enough.

He sat at the back, his little legs dangling innocently from the seat. His mind was in a complete daydream.

"Bears! Wow! I'll see bears!"

He had been looking forward to this day for months. He loved the wilderness and all natural things.

Once they had arrived, she filed them out and as the others ran off to see their favourites, he stayed by her side, holding her hand tightly.

She pushed him up to one of the cages. "Look at that, isn't it funny!"

He peered in.

A monkey gaily played, like a puppet on a string, leaping through hoops and applauding itself loudly.

"Well done, ooh, isn't it lovely, how sweet," she said, her eyes filled with joy; she felt amused.

"It doesn't seem real," he moaned. "More like a doll than an animal."

Moving on, she squealed with delight.

"Tigers, do you like tigers? Gosh. Come along now!"

Grabbing his hand even more tightly, she pulled him up to the enclosure. The tiger approached and opened its mouth, the black stripes on his back entangled together at his feet. Where a silver key stuck out, like a tree in a theme park, to wind him up.

"Hello young fellow, would you like a ride?"

The tiger grinned continuously, offering him a claw. He politely tugged at it.

"Come along, I don't bite. Tiggy, the friendly tiger, at your service." Wrenching himself free, he tore off. Away from her and away from the tiger.

Away from the glittering cages and the plastic smiles. Until he fell outside the gates of the place. On the floor, he noticed a hole which was invisible to those who had no eyes. He checked to see if anyone was looking.

"I wanna see the elephants."

"Just a minute, honey, I've just got to get a shot of that dancing hippo. Oh sugar, will you get me a happy face mask from the souvenir shop please? Thank you darling."

He was safe.

Tumbling to the bottom, he picked himself up. He rubbed his eyes and looked around. Letting out an enormous scream, he fell to the floor.

Sobbing.

His dreams shattered, broken, taken from him.

For he was surrounded by the bodies of a million creatures, all different shapes and sizes. Creatures which no longer made plastic masks smile, for these ones could not dance or talk, only cry. Cry, because their homes had been taken to make grey, dismal cities and money-making machines. Cry, because they had been used to amuse the bored, then thrown away when no longer needed.

Nowhere to live, their places taken by cardboard cut-outs, they lay, carcasses of the natural, victims of the briefcase.

He wiped his eyes. Gently pushing aside other bodies, he lay beside the body of a great bear, closer to himself than he had ever been.

Dreaming once again.

Apathy Of Ignorance

Up until then, they had sat in silence. Sipping cups of 'Tea Lover' in a non-smoking 'oxygen breathing only' zone saw to that. His eyelids were held down by iron bars. Her arms, legs and head were tied in a ridiculous knot. She felt proud – it was the new, the latest, 'crumple' look.

"Good job we're living now really." He spoke, his voice breaking a crystal 'don't chatter 'cos I shatter' window at the back of the room.

"Yes, dear, you're right as usual," she managed to grunt, pulling her head free from the rope that bound her mind.

Their isolated existence saw whitewashed walls and frilly skirts as being a world. A world in their minds, their world to everyone else. A red-laced curtain of ignorance hid all reality behind it.

The game of life was played, ignored, under their noses. People sang, suffered, resisted, starved and thought under the very table at which they sat. Hungry fists beat angrily at his feet, imprisoned hands pulled at their tablecloth, a megaphone even blasted rebel songs and rhythms of resistance directly, loudly, deliberately, into their ears.

But to them the room was silent. The banging fists were factory sirens, the moving tablecloth merely a waitress' clumsiness, and the rebel songs just the louder than usual drone of the unwatched radiation screen-vision.

"Good job really, I would hate to have lived a while ago. All that dirt I suppose." Unnoticed, the bundle of limbs had fallen off her chair.

Still now they sit, her scrambling tiredly to raise herself off the floor, him blinded by bars so that he can't see her, the both of them gagged by the rules.

And every day, the crystal window smashes a little nearer to their tea tray.

The End Of Youth

He looked out of the window. As the machine pulled up, he could see them coming. Teams of little black insects, scurrying frantically to board it.

Their briefcases glistened in the sunlight.

One by one they filed in, robotically, obediently, they sat down, pushing away others who sat in their seats. He saw his bag thrown aside by an insect who thrust his beetle-like body beside him. Bored, he took his bag from the floor and continued to watch from his front row seat, through the window. In a world of his own.

He was very young, too bored to be angry. Too tired to be bitter. Youth, energy, dreams and imagination had been sucked from him a long, long time ago. From birth he was created. An old man.

The machine started and they set off. Through the country. The cage was in complete silence except for the occasional bleep of a creature turning the pages of a magazine. Full to the brim of blank, white sheets.

He sighed: he knew that the cardboard trees weren't for real and that insects had no feelings. Expressionless, unemotional, blank, like sheets of paper, they stared falsely into closed space. He was weary, his arms dragging, sagging, drooping, by his side.

'This is a world of nothingness,' he thought. 'If I were to be murdered, not one of them would move. Not an inch.'

The machine stopped and they all got out.

Filed out, left to right, their briefcases glistening in the sunlight.

Lost Memories

He slammed the door. Once he had thrown his bags on the floor, he remembered. 'Four o'clock, by the school, don't forget.' He couldn't wait, he loved walking, especially that way. Hurriedly pulling on a worn mac, he searched the house for an umbrella. The rain spat at his cosy living room from the outside, inviting him out to join the fun.

The wind was blowing, so he decided 'an umbrella in the wind is as good as none at all,' as his grandmother put it.

Stepping out into the cold, gusty street, he checked his pocket.

The key was there, he tried putting it in the back of his jeans. A sharp pain shot through his right leg every time he lifted it. 'If it hurts, don't do it,' his grandmother would say. Placing the key in one shoe, he began the journey.

He enjoyed walking, even in the dark. Strolling alone at night was his favourite pastime. He adored the country and all its wonders, the wind gently breezing caringly across his face, the murmur of the trees as he passed and the for ever changing pattern of the clouds. Whenever he walked he could think, he could solve problems and talk to himself, without anyone being the wiser.

The school was situated over the other side of his estate. To get to it was 'quite a way, son', as his grandmother put it. As he went, he suddenly realised that the route he was taking was an old route, past his old house and the green where he used to play as a child. His heart beat faster and faster, like a wound-up drumming doll, excited so much by the thought of seeing childhood memories again. Quickly striding down alleys, running through thickets, he came to the old street, unchanged by years of wear. But he hadn't come to see the street. Closing his eyes, he carefully stepped and tiptoed along the pavement. His top teeth were firmly clamped over his upper lip to stop his teeth from chattering. Halting at the place where he knew the green was, he stood still. There was no one about: silence covered the road, blanketing the sound of children's play and screeching cars.

He opened his eyes, and all the joy and happiness he felt sank to the bottom of his now broken heart.

There was a block of flats, widely spread, all over the green play area, leaving not one blade of grass to show where it had once been.

Like Father Like Son

He was a handsome lad, not fat but well-built, definitely not skinny. He had a fine head of hair: black, thick and strongly rooted. His eyes were large and extraordinarily blue. They were deep-set and fixed a stare so vivid that all were enchanted.

His life was a social one: full of parties, drinking and, of course, girlfriends. He would get up in the afternoon, take pills for a hangover then set out for the next party.

On a cold day, probably in winter, this young man decided to take a walk, perhaps to sober up just before a 'bit of a do' which a good friend of his was throwing.

The people he knew thought he was certainly an odd one. Sure as that the old woman from number twenty-two would remark: "Ah, there's none so queer as folk." But this night, no one saw him. He made quite sure of that.

There was a narrow thicket by the street where he lived. A small lane where he had first encountered real fear as a child. The wind ran her fingers through his hair as the snow fell, kissing his shoulders and face with an icy sparkle. Approaching the lane, he felt warm; he was wearing no coat, nor gloves, yet he felt warm, not hot. It was here he began, trailing his hand through the hedgerow of the narrow lane. He danced with the snow and hugged each tree with a tenderness more loving than he had ever felt before. On turning from this, his eyes lit up, those blue eyes dazzling with excitement. For in a pile, beneath an old oak lay thousands of fallen leaves, raked together, dying together. Glancing briefly around him to make sure that no one could see, he dived in, tossing leaf after leaf. Leaves became people, stones formed houses, earth became food and in less than an instant, he was wallowing in a dreamy paradise surrounded by friends, food and home.

A rustle in the hedge behind him said that someone had seen him. Whom, he could not tell. Everything was transformed back to its real form. He sat alone, quite damp, seated in a mud throne, amongst the pile of decaying leaves.

He Knows Best

She looks around herself. Neatly arranged, gold-bound mini-Shakespeares line the shelves. Next to the china teapots, six porcelain cats work their way down the mantelpiece. The largest one at the top and so on.

In the centre, the television stands with accompanying video. It takes prime position in the living room, it is her only source of human activity, her only contact with the outside world.

She doesn't know why she feels sorry for herself. He's bought her everything a woman could dream of: a high-tech washer-drier, Chanel No. 5, an all-in-one fridge freezer and even a compact iron and ironing board which, when neatly folded, fits nicely into the side of the drinks cabinet.

He takes good care of her. He makes sure that she doesn't go out on her own, but occasionally allows her down to the club with him on a Monday night. As long as she looks presentable. Yes she really is quite lucky. A good man.

She glances at the piano, remembering how she'd wondered why they had a piano if no one was to play it. She had longed to play but he'd had to explain to her. She wasn't as clever. She couldn't play the piano because he didn't want her to overwork herself, what with the housework and all. Now she understood, it was obvious.

Anyway he didn't have the money to throw around on piano lessons. He always had the answer to everything, though. The next day he brought home a satellite dish.

"Now you won't have an excuse to go out with the girls," he laughed.

And she saw her reflection in the glass.

Arachnophobia

Delicately she stepped. Silently, she crossed the shadowed corner wall so that she would not be noticed. Her eight small feet touched the plaster with the grace and the elegance of a dancer. Silvery threads of beauty wove her home into the evening quiet.

Cursing and swearing, they glared at her.

"Disgusting."

"Ugly."

"Kill her."

Affecting nobody, she rid the room of the pests that they hated, the diseases that they would contract, the dirt that they would accumulate. Her well-planned web grew thick, like an ever-strengthening forest, with the remains of yesterday's dinner. It was time for her to move on.

"Ugh."

"Disgusting."

"Ugly."

Taking her time, she began to move. Each leg placed so tenderly to make sure that she was safe. Her head turned for a moment and she noticed them, raising their hands in the air. With the hatred of one united bigot.

And her world collapsed about her.

The Progression Of The Road

She looked at it. Gazing at the branches that welcomed her lovingly to sit beneath it. She knelt down; never in her life had she smelt a scent so fresh as the aroma around her. The greenness blinded her with its richness, the strong branches sheltered her from wind. And rain. For day upon day she would lie upon this creation of nature. Many a flashing light and polluting machine would pull at her clothes and hair with their iron claws, but she resisted. Her only pleasure was just to be with the greenery.

"You're mad," her friends would say, telling their children not to befriend her and to play army games 'like other kids'. And still she strayed, not alone and quite, in fact very, happy.

Each day, another branch would grow and people started to become interested. The iron claws were thrown away as they became excited by the fun and enjoyment which could be had by being together. So, in a short while, there was quite a collection. Old, young, men, women – all gathered. She invited them to smell nature's perfume with her and the branches extended to form arms that kept them from cold weather and wind.

Then, one day, a machine arrived. In one hand it held a bunch of guns, flickering screens and polluting mobiles that murdered the aroma with each puff. In the other it held a silver blade that glistened, like an iron claw, in the sunlight. Advancing steadily, it grinned, handing the children guns and screens whilst adults were dragged from their places by the mobiles that rendered their feet useless. It carried on until all were gone, except her, lying, clinging on to the tree of life. As the blade cut, she screamed, her eyes filled with tears, pleading for mercy. But no one could hear her: they were all watching flickering screens and playing with guns.

Down it fell, her still clinging and shouting wildly, until she was silenced by its dying arms.

And then it was taken, abused and burned by the machine which pulled its admirers away.

The Tear

She only arrived this morning. Not with the post exactly, but soon after it. He picked up the mail and selected his own letters. Acting 'the postman' for his house, he delivered the rest. "Hey J—, there's a letter here for you."

Tripping over an old coffee cup, he stumbled into his bedroom and sat on the bed, opening the post. Rip. The first was a printed bill. "Two hundred and forty quid," he said.

"I never used as much electricity as that."

"You did," called a voice from the other room.

"You and that bloody tape recorder! I'll chuck you out one of these days."

Rip. A small piece of paper fell out. The cheque made him smile. "I could do with that," he sighed and put it aside.

She was waiting for the opening of the letter which lay at the bottom of the heap. She didn't think that he had even noticed her, waiting. Just waiting for him to open it.

Rip. The birthday card. From Aunty E— of course. Rip. A birthday greeting from Uncle George and his nephew Phil. Granny and Grandad put in an appearance too.

"To the tune of fifty pounds and a beautiful watch," he grinned. Rip, rip, rip. They all opened one by one until...

Rip. She was reading, waiting for the thud as the lightweight paper hit the floor. To match the sound of his heart.

Following the words across the handwritten page, his eyes began to fill.

I'm sorry, I'm really sorry but—

He cut himself off from the words and threw the paper on the ground.

Glistening like a silver pearl, she trickled down his face. Lovingly. Soothing and reassuring, she told him in a salty stutter that he would be all right. She ran, or rather paced quite freely and tried to comfort him as she went, talking, sighing, helping. Till he brushed her away with one swipe of his hand.

False Affection

They scolded her when she played in the mud.

"Get out! Girls don't get dirty."

They frowned when she laughed and scorned her gaiety.

"You may laugh," they said. "But where's my dinner?"

Stone like bars prevented her from leaving the house: a prisoner of boredom, she looked out of the window.

"You may look," they said. "But where's my shirt?"

Each day she became more restless and so she began to read, a book she had found on a shelf nearby.

'If I read', she thought, 'I can learn'

And so she sat, day after day, until she was discovered by them, envious of her knowledge.

"I don't think you'll be reading any more, you can use this," indicating a large poisonous screen they had fitted in the corner of her room.

One day, after the pub, they came home. She had prepared food, and their spoons were set so that she could spoon-feed each one, if she ran very fast around the table. They didn't know where their fingers were.

"I've brought you a present," they said, patting her on the head.

"There's no need to thank me." They smiled, nearly falling in generosity from their monumental orange box pillars of kindness.

"Go on, open it, you're allowed."

A hand helped her to undo the wrapping.

Unfolding back the brown, soft, giving wrapping paper, she realised what it was.

A small pink box with the words 'I LOVE YOU' engraved carefully on the front.

Tradition

She began to sing. Looking around the room, all she could see in front of her were blank faces. The entire room had fallen silent; they had all quietened simultaneously, so that she could sing.

Her voice was not trained at all in any way, yet it was beautiful. It flowed, like running water, from her mouth, the lyrics telling of mountains and rivers, places she loved. When the song was over she sat back in her chair. A resounding echo of the joy in her was reflected in the eyes of all the people in the room. They clapped and whistled, asking once more for 'another one'. On refusing, the music started up again. People scraped madly on old violins, blew their hearts out of rusty penny whistles, laughed heartily to the beat of the drum and played traditional music, together.

The chatter was high all the time: people spoke of their families, jobs and home. Tongues gaily wagged in the native language; no need for a ring to specify a speaker. The language of the people was the mother tongue of the country. There was dancing, music, talking, food, jokes. They were all enjoying themselves, together.

Then one day, amidst the merriment and song, the room once more fell silent. But not for a song. This was a deadly silence, not an excited one, but one of fear. It stood at the door, a collection of wooden sticks in Its hand, waiting for the attention of all.

She winced, bravely, as she held out her hand. The cane was strict, as were the rules. They were each in possession of a wooden stick on which a notch was marked every time they danced, sang or spoke.

It glanced briefly about the room. The cane in Its grasp trembled and shook, like a man trying to balance a pitchfork on his head. It wasn't powerful, It was frightened. Scared stiff of the dancing shoes and wooden bows. Songs of tradition kept It from sleeping at night, and the speaking of native tongue had bitten Its nails down to the bone. Such terrible thoughts ran through Its head. What if one were to discover the power of a fiddle? One scrape and It would be finished, dead, stamped out.

Her hands were scarred from the rule of the cane, her throat sore from the lack of speaking. She felt tired of not enjoying herself. Others were feeling the same. Her head was heavy, her heart not a lot higher. She decided that she'd had enough. They all faced It, cornered It.

Staring It straight in the eye, she opened her mouth.

Lost Love

It was a small box that she found. A tiny wooden crate painted black, with a little keyhole and the words 'LEAVE ME ALONE' written on the side.

A key was lying beside it. Picking it up, she put it curiously into the lock. Click. She felt it turning, turning, almost spinning in the lock: a great discoverer, she lifted the lid.

Inside lay a jumbled heap of rubbish; watches, a piece of string, nails and a torn envelope.

"Hmm, nothing of value," she said, leafing through the pages of a scribbled diary.

'Can't even write legibly,' she thought.

Rummaging in that box was silly: so many worthless items, so many useless artefacts. She giggled, and stopped laughing. A photograph, brown, torn, but still recognisable, lay at the bottom of the pile.

Lifting it out, she smiled. He was happy-looking, green-grey eyes twinkling brightly above a beautiful array of white teeth. Long brown hair covered his small shoulders. 'Petit and loving, happy and bored,' she thought. 'Everything that is the norm. I'm glad he's that way.'

The wind blew and the box rattled its contents. Hurriedly, she put back the photograph, replaced all the other items and put the box, closed with the key beside it, out of sight. Being childish, for she was a child, she hid.

He arrived soon enough. Finding the box immediately, he opened it and gazed at the photo. Touching each possession as if it were his own, he started as she stepped out.

"I touched it, I know I shouldn't have."

Apologetically, she lowered her eyes.

"I'm sorry."

He looked at her and spoke, his eyes filling slowly with uncared for tears.

"It isn't mine," he said.

Animal Madness

She lifted her head.

"Go on." She knew that she had to move some time. Pushing aside two friendly hens, she got out of her chair.

"Let's take you out then," she said, taking the bounding animal out of the place.

The day was dreary, the clouds murmured in constant conference, muttering darkly about the howling wind. She managed to drag herself a few steps, listening to the trees and watching the wildlife. Rover bounced on ahead, his tongue out, sliding down muddy lanes and letting the wind blow coolly through his long black fur.

Her feet were tired after a while; they ached. "Blasted things," she said and tied up the laces.

At last they came to the special place. Rover darted in amongst the woodland, shaking hands with the squirrels and hugging the birds. She sat herself down feeling quite contented, and read a story.

It was not long afterwards when she heard the sound. It was strange; she couldn't quite make it out.

'The best way to describe this sound, is... no sound,' she thought. A silence blanketed the ground, the birds stopped their song, the insects stopped their clicking, the fox, the deer, the squirrels had all gone. And Rover.

Searching frantically, she pushed branches away from her, yet they made no sound. Pulling back hedges, kicking back leaves, she screamed, "ROVER!" But no noise could be heard.

A door swung open and she stepped inside. The noise was deafening. Rows of tiny cages were stacked on top of one another, each containing five or six animals. Treading on and biting each other, they squawked. But the man in the suit could not hear them. Walking on, she saw young calves unable to move, whilst as they lay still a hungry thing gnawed at their legs. Monkeys gazed at her with no eyes, their brains in test tubes, bleeding boringly.

'Rabbits cannot cry,' she thought, 'so they can't ever be unhappy.'

Neither can rats, yet the tears flooded the room in her presence. A rusty pig hung upside down, it looked at her and sighed, "Roast pork tonight, is it?"

She slammed the door.

"Ughh! Disgusting! I'm glad it doesn't happen here." Hurrying out of the forest, she bustled up the street.

"Ughh! Disgusting! I'm glad it doesn't happen here."

Until her attention was attracted to a small transparent plastic bag lying beneath a lamp-post, the words 'delicious dainty drummer sticks, the finest chicken' written on the front. The legs were still inside, attached somewhere to a tortured hen. And she realised that Rover had vanished for ever.

Servant's Shoes

Her eyes followed the raindrops as they drizzled carelessly down the window. Drop by drop, she stared at the metallic glow of each one. Following them right down to her feet.

Her feet. Two worn work machines, wearied to their utmost capacity by other people's laundry, other people's food, by other children's parents.

The shoes that she was wearing were faded and moth-eaten. He had offered to buy her another pair, expensive, the best. At first she had consented, but, well, they reminded her of her home. The yellow stripes were symbolic of the morning sun rays, the red circles were her mother's home cooking, the green slashes grew shoots of loveliness in the garden of her home.

So she kept them.

Home. She thought of it. The friends whom she knew and had left behind, her own small bed, the smell of bread in the oven. Waiting for her to eat it.

Her mother, whose precious tears fell daily for the little girl she had lost, her own child, so very far away.

Thinking like this was bad for her. She felt angry, yet with a sense of hopelessness, she rose to the sound of a bell with a start. It was the beginning of yet another day in the middle of one of many, many weeks.

"These are getting quite worn," she said. And threw the shoes away.

The Prisoner

He felt the pain of a hard stick, prodding and poking his back, as, blindfolded, he was led away. The machines at his side rattled furiously, shouting and ordering, with authority which they didn't have.

The dark room lit up as he entered. No saintly light, but a light of humanity from his eyes permitted him to see the scrawlings of previous prisoners. Harmless notes such as '*I woz here, were you?*' engraved deeply into the walls. Others, perhaps not so friendly, screamed out of frustration and anger. Some had written what, to him, was poetry: articulate, eloquent, quite beautiful, yet it thumped, inelegantly, through his head. Powerfully.

He took his seat on a grey bench. How he could tell its colour, I don't know, for it was pitch-black. Fumbling blindly, his hands searched for a pillow; finding nothing, they returned to his forehead where they soothed his mind.

A large, hairy, rodent-like creature scuttled across his foot. Handcuffed and chained, it stumbled past, unaware of his presence. He bent down and touched it: the animal's fur was warm and soft. How kind the hated rat must have been to give a man such comfort. He decided that no longer would he use 'rat' as an insult.

The room was cold, his feet were frozen. Loneliness bit its knife-like jaws at him, into him. How long can you last on your own? He questioned, interrogated himself and prepared a lengthy speech for his release. Talking first to the wall, then to the bed and finally to his feet (which he considered no longer a part of himself) he realised that he was going insane.

One quick move and it would end. He contemplated dying but it didn't appeal. After all, the rat had survived. Having less strength than a rodent made him feel small.

The door of the room opened. She walked in, her figure resembling his. Sitting down, she smiled. Her eyes showed the spirit of a fighter and, for the first time, he opened his.

He was not alone.

Censorship

Click click. The keys of a typewriter tapping their war-torn tune.
He sat sweating, the remains of old articles strewn about the room.
'Take twenty,' he thought and began again.

But they didn't like what he wrote. From their six foot stools,
they looked down.

"You must be objective, young man."

"Intolerance is not a virtue, you know, so stop this disobedience."

The keys clicked. He wrote more, about hidden things. His face,
in a tired grimace, revealed all that they were concealing.

His home was full of paper. It filled his study, his living room,
and even his kitchen. At the end of each article he would chop a
centimetre off their stools, off the bottom of their stools. Until their
wigs trailed, exposed and defeated, along the floor.

Tears of anguish trickled down their faces. Their cronies, dirty
job-doers, watchdogs, rushed about, to and fro, trying to capture the
man. But, as soon as they reached his house, they would hear him
clicking ten miles away. The watchdogs danced and danced, yet the
stools were getting shorter.

Then, in a fit of rage, a man in a wig cut the watchdogs' strings.
The dogs fell to the floor, motionless, unable to function.

Click click. He had five typewriters all smashing the crystal of
censorship at the same time.

A knock at the door; he turned the handle. The judges did their
job. They still had their strings.

And the journalist reached, with groping arms, for his typewriter
through the bars of a cage.